"Cindy Lou Ella"

A Country

Fairy Tale

Cindy Lou Ella ... A Country Fairy Tale©

Cindy Lou Ella ... A Country Fairy Tale©

I.SBN: 978-1-933660-28-8
(HARDCOVER)

Printed in China

A Publishing Division of Smooth Sailing Press
PO Box 1439 / Tomball, Texas 77377
SAN# 257-2680

This book is lovingly dedicated to my husband Gavin.

Thank you for being my biggest fan and for believing in me always. You inspire me!

To my sister and friend Samantha...I love you!

The laughter and good times we have shared are the best a sister could ever ask for.

To my grandmother Josie who always watched us drive away by peeking around the curtain.

Now you are watching us from heaven. You are our angel.

Once upon a time on a small farm down in Texas,

there lived a little country girl as sweet as molasses.

Her name was Cindy Lou Ella, with her long hair like pure spun gold.

She was her Daddy Earl's pride and joy, even now at eighteen years old.

Her momma Darlene had gone on to be with the Lord when Cindy Lou Ella was just a little girl.

Then her Daddy soon remarried to a mean old woman named Katy Pearl.

Now, Katy Pearl had two daughters that were as mean as an old bull on a scorching hot day in July.

Their names were Sissy Lynn and Reba Sue, and their specialty was making poor Cindy Lou Ella Cry.

Cindy Lou Ella always had the feeling that her stepmother and stepsisters wanted her out of the way.

They always made her do all of the daily chores so that she would not have the time to play.

"Milk the cows, slop the hogs and gather up all of the eggs!

Scrub the floors, wash the clothes and don't *even* whine about your aching legs!"

All of these orders and demands Katy Pearl would boldly shout.

She would keep piling chores on Cindy Lou Ella until she would wear that girl plum out!

Daddy Earl never even knew any of this meanness towards Cindy Lou Ella was going on.

He had taken to his bed real sick and was as weak as a tiny fawn.

Cindy Lou Ella didn't want to worry her precious Daddy, so she never uttered a word.

When she would bring him his supper in the evening she would tell him to rest assured.

That she was so very happy and that Katy Pearl and the girls were so kind.

She knew that if her Daddy ever knew the truth he would just about lose his mind.

She would lovingly sit by his bed and read to him from his favorite book

and Earl would just stare at his daughter and the care that she took.

To be with him through all of his pain and not have a life of her own,

he wanted her to get married and have her own little home.

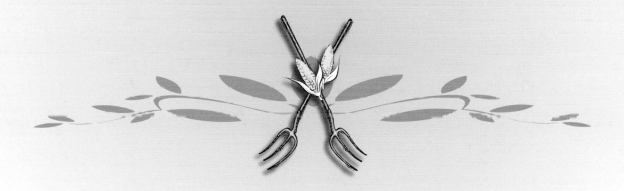

As Cindy Lou Ella would tend to the fields on her Daddy's old tractor

she would dream of having her own home too, about living… "happily ever after."

On the other side of town, where life is for the rich and frilly,

There lived a handsome young man and his name was Joe Billy.

He was the sole heir to a fortune and never knew what it was like to be poor.

He was guaranteed to inherit his Daddy's flourishing tractor parts store.

His Daddy, Joe Billy, Sr. told him that it was time for him to find a purty little wife.

He was going to throw a special shindig as early as tomorrow night.

"Who is going to help you run the store when your mamma and I aren't here?

You could have any gal in town that you wanted; they will come from far and near.

Just to have one dance with my handsome son Joe Billy and maybe catch his eye forever.

She needs to be sweet, she needs to be classy and it wouldn't hurt if she was clever."

Joe Billy replied, "I know every gal in town and not a one of them I would want to marry.

The thought of being hitched to one is down right scary.

But I'll let you give this dance and we will sure as fire see

if it's my money that they want, or just to be with me."

The announcement went out the next day on the AM radio

That this very night there would be a dance next to the old drive-in show.

It said for all of the ladies to come to the Old Town Hall,

It started at nine and to be on time and don't forget your dancin' boots, ya'll!

Sissy Lynn and Reba Sue were painting each other's nails

When they heard the announcement and Reba Sue started to wail...

"Oh my gosh, what in the world am I going to wear to this special little dance?

My black starched jeans or my hot pink leather pants?"

They both started rummaging through their closets and their drawers,

when all of the sudden they heard a soft knock on their door.

"What is going on in there?" Cindy Lou Ella innocently wanted to know.

Sissy Lynn yanked open the door and yelled, "Don't you have some flowers to grow?"

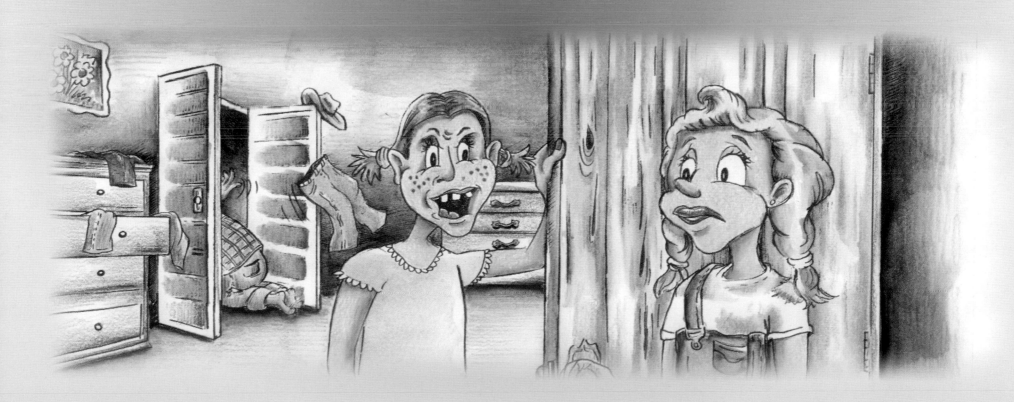

"You know Mamma told you to get to work in the yard!"

And that is when Cindy Lou Ella started to bawl real hard.

She tore off running to the meadow behind the old red barn.

She threw herself down into bluebonnets and buried her head in her arms.

When she finally had no more tears because they had all run bone dry,

She sat up and looked around and boy was she surprised!

Because there right in front of her had to be the oddest thing she had ever seen.

There was a opossum in a pink cowboy hat and she announced, "I am your fairy godmother, Pearlene!"

Standing right beside her was an armadillo in a dress.

"I am your other fairy godmother Adel and we will get you out of this mess!"

Cindy Lou Ella replied, "Why, what mess are you talking about? I don't quite understand."

Pearlene boasted, "Why that hoedown going on tonight, we're going to help you find a man!"

"Quiet down, Pearlene" Adel said gently.

"You honestly sound like an old hillbilly.

There is a dance tonight, my precious one.

We are going to dress you up. You need to have some fun.

Those sisters of yours have been mean to you for the very last time."

"Now sit up child," Pearlene piped in, "Your fashion is all mine!"

"Not so fast, Pearlene – your fashion is a little much.

Let me give her a gentle touch."

With the flip of Adel's wand made of lace,

Cindy Lou Ella became dressed with impeccable taste.

Her dress was light pink with pretty little pink cowboy boots to match

And Pearlene hollered "Oooohweee, now all you need is a sparkly cowboy hat!"

With the flip of her wand made of purple leather,

She whistled and said, "Now that is much better."

Cindy Lou Ella twirled all around

She felt like she was being lifted up off of the ground.

To dance would make her feel great

and then she stopped suddenly and said, "Oh wait!"

"My stepsisters probably took the truck to the dance,

and they would never give me the chance to ride with them into town."

And then Cindy Lou Ella could not help but frown.

Adel said, "Girl, there is nothing to fear when Pearlene and I are here.

Our diesel truck is behind the barn, We'll drive you there, but please be forewarned

Pearlene drives a little fast!"

And with that said, they were gone in a flash!

Pearlene took the curves on the gravel road like she was a racecar driver on the track.

Pearlene said, "Don't be scared sugar, we'll get you there safely and that's a fact."

The truck rolled up to the dance hall in a cloud of smoke and dust.

Pearlene said, "Take this card and in the message you must trust."

Cindy Lou Ella looked down. The business card plainly said,

"Don't for a second take that cowboy hat off of your head.

For if you do, the magic of the night will be totally broken.

The Rags to Riches Fairy Godmother Company has spoken."

When Cindy Lou Ella looked up, the two creatures of the night were gone

and in that moment she heard her favorite song.

She entered the front door and a hush fell over the crowd,

Joe Billy wondered what was happening, and then he turned around.

He found himself staring and didn't want to make a scene,

but he knew in that instant that he had found his country queen.

He made his way through the crowd to her and asked, "May I please have the honor of this dance?"

Cindy Lou Ella did not hesitate; she knew this was her big chance.

They two-stepped through the night and spun across the floor.

The other people in the room did not seem to matter anymore.

It was like they were the only ones left in the room

And Joe Billy said, "I hope tonight is not it. I must see you again soon."

Cindy Lou Ella replied, "I honestly feel just the same, but you haven't even told me your name."

"Well my name is Joe Billy and my daddy gave this dance just for me.

He wanted me to find a wife here and I just couldn't see

how I'd ever find someone to be with forever that would be so pure and true.

But, I know that I have found her, now that I'm with you."

Suddenly the dance hall door flung open and a strong summer wind rushed in.

Cindy Lou Ella's hat flew off and she remembered Pearlene's words again.

Before Joe Billy even realized what was going on

Cindy Lou Ella ran out of the dance hall and just like a ghost she was gone.

The sound of a diesel truck was clanking over on the street.

As Cindy Lou Ella ran to it, she noticed her bare feet!

The cowboy hat was gone, her jeans were on and so was her old worn t-shirt.

She looked tattered, her dreams were shattered and above all her feelings were hurt.

Adel said, "Get on up in this truck dear girl and hold on real tight!

The Rags to Riches magical spell has been broken for tonight!"

Pearlene punched the gas and they were off down the old gravel road.

Pearlene turned to Adel and shouted, "We are getting way too old!"

Suddenly Cindy Lou Ella started to cry and Adel looked her square in the eye

and said, "Don't cry Cindy Lou Ella, we just know things will work out for you."

"Life always works out for the good people in the end.

Just remember, we are not only your fairy godmothers, but your true friends."

They wheeled up to the back of the barn and Cindy Lou Ella slowly got out of the truck.

Pearlene and Adel both hugged her and whispered, "Good luck."

With that said, they both jumped back into the truck and peeled out of sight.

Cindy Lou Ella sauntered back to the house and thought, "Golly what a night!"

She tiptoed through the house and then snuggled up in bed.

She dreamed of Joe Billy and all that he had said.

On the other side of town, up and not able to go to bed,

was the handsome Joe Billy with visions of Cindy Lou Ella in his head.

"I don't even know where she lives, or the sound of her name.

I have got to find her tomorrow or I will go insane!"

The only thing he had of hers was the pink cowboy hat.

He held it close to his heart and thought, "Well, that settles that!"

From house to house he went and placed the cowboy hat on many a girl, but it did not fit.

He drove up to one last farm and thought to himself, "Well this is it."

He walked up to the porch and knocked on the old screen door.

He was beginning to think that this whole mission didn't matter anymore.

Katy Pearl opened the door and asked, "Well, what can we do for you?"

Joe Billy said, "I must have every girl in your house try on this hat to find my love so true."

Katy Pearl yelled, "Sissy Lynn, Reba Sue come here and don't take your time."

When Reba Sue saw the hat she yelled, "That is mine! That is mine!"

She quickly grabbed the hat and placed it on her head,

but it wouldn't go down far enough and her face turned hot and red.

Sissy Lynn grabbed it and put it on, but it fell down below her eyes.

At that moment Cindy Lou Ella walked in and boy was she surprised!

Katy Pearl saw the look exchanged between the boy and Cindy Lou.

Joe Billy gently placed the hat on her head and said, "Yee-haw, it is you!"

Katy Pearl snatched the hat off of Cindy Lou Ella and said,

"Well, I don't know what to say

but your Daddy Earl has never met this boy

and would never give you away."

At that moment they heard a voice clear

and turned around to see,

Daddy Earl was in the doorway

and he said, "Well, I'll be!

"My Cindy Lou Ella has found someone

that brings a smile to her face.

I without a doubt

give ya'll my approval and grace."

Right that second,

Joe Billy picked up Cindy Lou Ella

and swung her around

and a few months later,

Cindy Lou Ella was standing at the alter

in a gorgeous wedding gown.

Everyone was there, Katy Pearl, the sisters and Daddy Earl standing proud.

When Cindy Lou Ella was leaving the church she looked out into the crowd.

Everyone was so happy for them as they rushed out into the sun.

They were ready to go back to the dance hall, kick up their heels,

eat some barbeque and have some fun!

The truck waiting to take them to the hall had a familiar clanking sound that Cindy Lou Ella knew.

The tinted window slowly rolled down and Pearlene in shades said, "You-hoo!"

Cindy Lou Ella and Joe Billy jumped into the back seat and Cindy Lou Ella said, "Honey hold on tight!"

Adel yelled out, "Punch it, Pearlene" as they raced out of sight.

Well, that's the story of two country kids who fell in love, that is it and that is all.

And I'm bettin' they lived happily ever after... Now, don't ya'll?